Stargazers

by Michèle Dufresne
Illustrations by Tatjana Mai-Wyss

PIONEER VALLEY
EDUCATIONAL PRESS

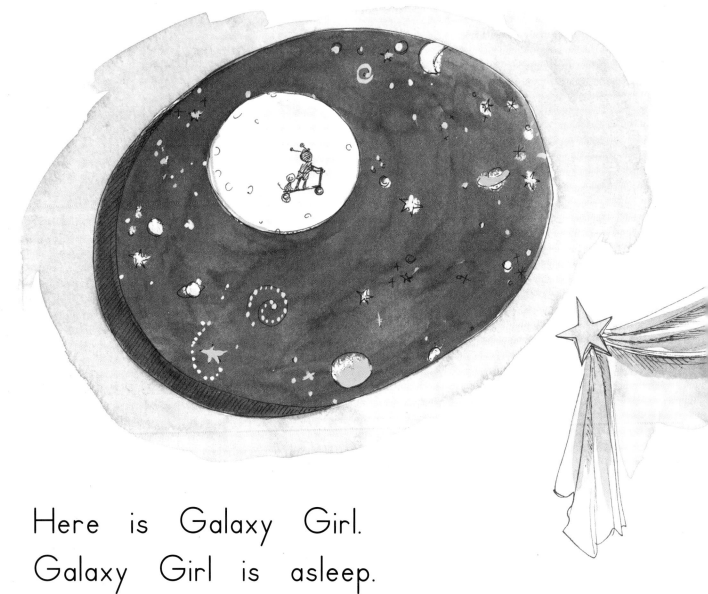

Here is Galaxy Girl.
Galaxy Girl is asleep.

2

Here is Spaceboy.
Spaceboy is up.

"Wake up, Galaxy Girl," said Spaceboy.

"I am asleep," said Galaxy Girl.

"Wake up! Wake up!" said Spaceboy.
"No," said Galaxy Girl. "I am asleep."

"Wake up, Galaxy Girl," said Spaceboy.

"No!" said Galaxy Girl.

"I am asleep!"

"Wake up, Galaxy Girl.
Look at the stars," said Spaceboy.

"OK," said Galaxy Girl. "I am up."

"Look at the stars," said Spaceboy.

"Wow!" said Galaxy Girl.
"Look at the stars!"